WHERE JESUS SLEPT

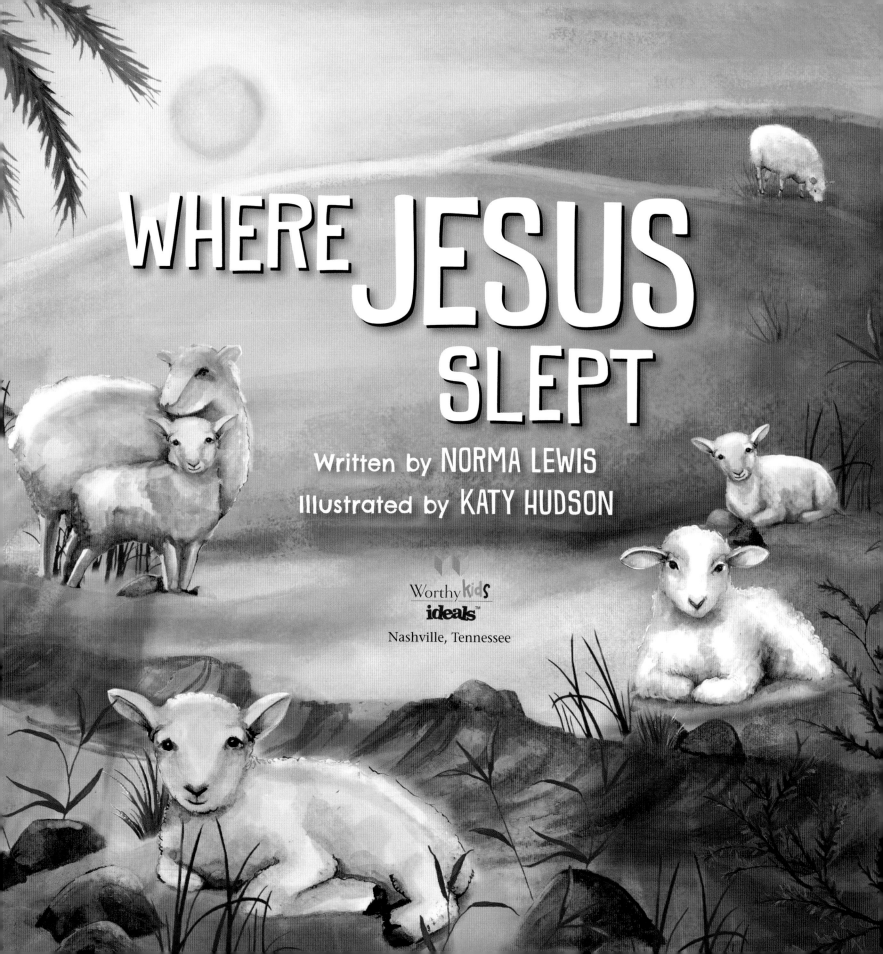

WHERE JESUS SLEPT

Written by NORMA LEWIS

Illustrated by KATY HUDSON

Worthy kids
ideals™

Nashville, Tennessee

ISBN-13: 978-0-8249-5679-0

Published by WorthyKids/Ideals
An imprint of Worthy Publishing Group
A division of Worthy Media, Inc.
Nashville, Tennessee

Text copyright © 2016 by Norma Lewis
Art copyright © 2016 by Katy Hudson

Scripture quotation on page 5 is from the *Holy Bible*, New Living Translation. Copyright
© 1996, 2004, 2007, 2013 by Tyndale House Foundation. Used by permission of Tyndale
House Publishers Inc., Carol Stream, Illinois 60188. All rights reserved.

    Scripture quotation on page 32 is from the *Holy Bible*, New International Version®,
NIV®. Copyright © 1973, 1978, 1984, 2011 by Biblica, Inc.® Used by permission of Zonder-
van. All rights reserved worldwide.

Library of Congress CIP data on file

Designed by Georgina Chidlow

Printed and bound in China
RRD-SZ_Jul16_1

For my grandson Shane.
I love you and I'm proud of you.
                              —N.L.
For my bridesmaids
Li, Lu, Brigs, Rach, and Wallen
                              —K.H.

I bring you good news that will bring great joy to all people. The Savior—yes, the Messiah, the Lord—has been born today in Bethlehem, the city of David!"

—LUKE 2:10B–11

Long, long ago,
in a city called Bethlehem,
a very special baby was born. . . .

This is the BED
where JESUS slept.

This is the **STRAW**
that lined the **BED**
where **JESUS** slept.

This is the COW
that shared the STRAW

that lined the BED
where JESUS slept.

This is the STABLE
that sheltered the COW

that shared the **STRAW**
that lined the **BED**
where **JESUS** slept.

This is MARY
there in the STABLE

that sheltered the COW
that shared the STRAW
that lined the BED
where JESUS slept.

This is the CHILD
all swaddled tight
born to MARY
there in the STABLE

that sheltered the COW
that shared the STRAW
that lined the BED
where JESUS slept.

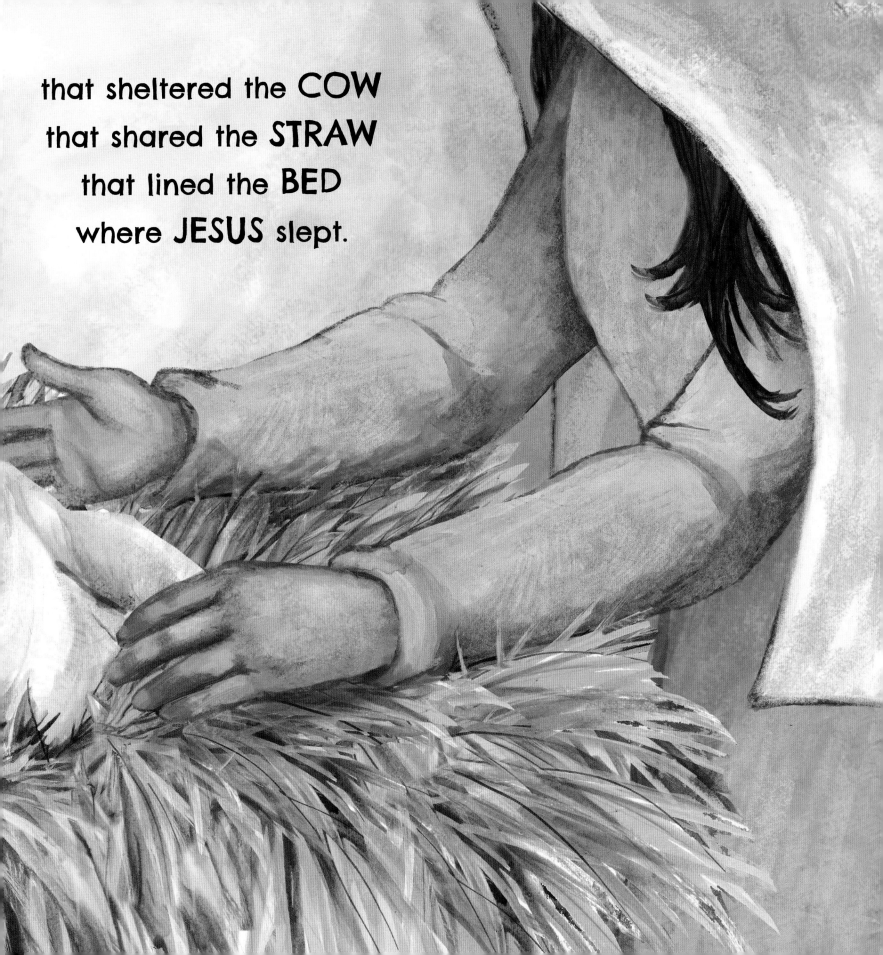

This is the ANGEL robed in white
that told of the CHILD
all swaddled tight

born to **MARY** there in the **STABLE**
that sheltered the **COW**
that shared the **STRAW**
that lined the **BED**
where **JESUS** slept.

This is the LAMB
that quaked at the sight
of the holy ANGEL robed in white

that told of the **CHILD** all swaddled tight

born to **MARY** there in the **STABLE**

that sheltered the **COW**

that shared the **STRAW**

that lined the **BED**

where **JESUS** slept.

This is the SHEPHERD who on that night
tended the LAMB that
quaked at the sight
of the holy ANGEL
robed in white
that told of the CHILD
all swaddled tight

born to MARY there in the STABLE
that sheltered the COW
that shared the STRAW
that lined the BED
where JESUS slept.

This is the STAR
  that was shining bright
above the SHEPHERD who on that night
tended the LAMB that quaked at the sight
of the holy ANGEL robed in white
that told of the CHILD all swaddled tight

born to MARY there in the STABLE
that sheltered the COW
that shared the STRAW
that lined the BED
where JESUS slept.

These are the WISE MEN
who followed the light
of the heavenly STAR
shining bright
above the SHEPHERD
who on that night
tended the LAMB
that quaked at the sight
of the holy ANGEL robed in white

that told of the CHILD

all swaddled tight

born to MARY

there in the STABLE

that sheltered the COW

that shared the STRAW

that lined the BED

where JESUS slept.

"These are the GIFTS
    for our KING tonight,"
said the three WISE MEN
    who followed the light
of the heavenly STAR shining bright
above the SHEPHERD
who on that night
tended the LAMB
that quaked at the sight
of the holy ANGEL
robed in white
that told of the CHILD
all swaddled tight

born to MARY there in the STABLE
that sheltered the COW
that shared the STRAW
that lined the BED
where JESUS slept.

Long, long ago,
in a city called Bethlehem,
a very special baby was born.
He was the Son of God!

His name was Jesus,
and God sent Him because
He loves us very much.

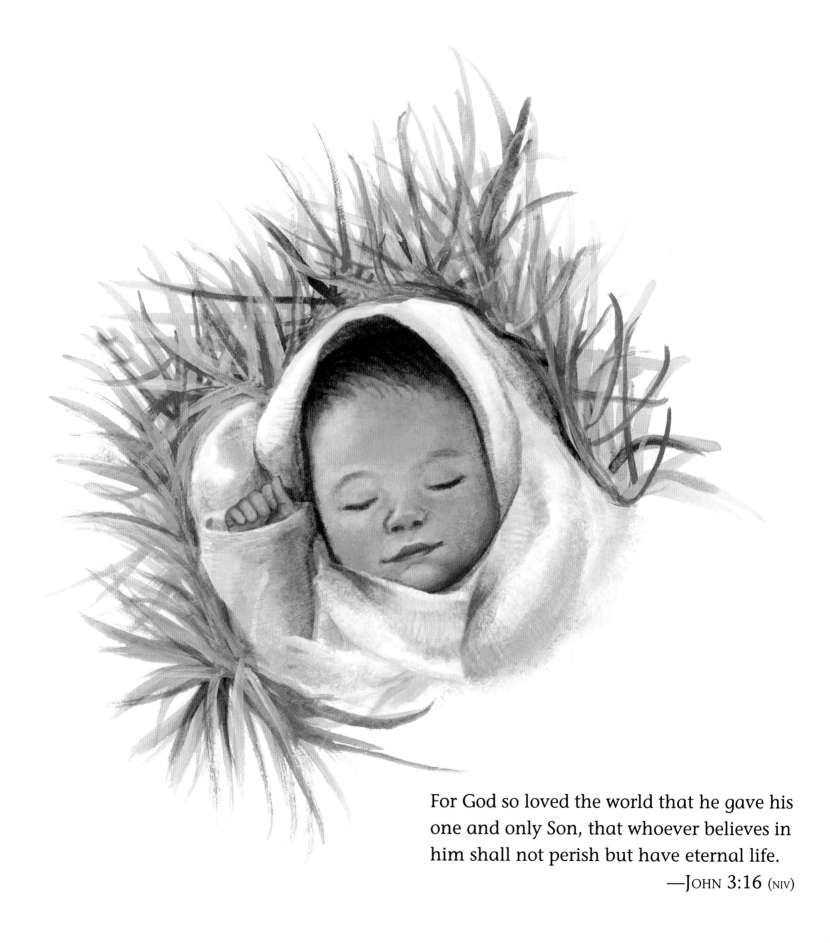

For God so loved the world that he gave his one and only Son, that whoever believes in him shall not perish but have eternal life.

—John 3:16 (NIV)